KT-523-844

The Story of Rumpelstiltskin

LONDON BOROUGH OF
HACKNEY
LIBRARY SERVICES

LOCAT	CLA
ACC. NO.	
CLASS	

Retold by Heather Amery
Illustrated by Stephen Cartwright

Language consultant: Betty Root
Series editor: Jenny Tyler

There's a little yellow duck to find on every page.

LONDON BOROUGH OF HACKNEY
3 8040 01224 9431

This poor miller has a very clever daughter.

He boasts about her. "Sire, my daughter is so clever that she can even spin straw into gold," he tells the King.

The King takes the daughter to his palace.

He shows her a room with some straw and a spinning wheel.
"Spin it into gold by morning, or you'll die," he says.

The daughter sits down and cries.

She can't spin straw into gold. Then a little man comes in.
"What will you give me if I spin it for you?" he asks.

"I'll give you my necklace," she says.

The little man spins away all night. By morning, he has spun all the straw into gold thread. Then he disappears.

The King is very pleased with the gold.

He shows the daughter another room with more straw.

"Spin that into gold by morning, or you'll die," he says.

Soon the little man comes in.

"What will you give me if I spin this bigger pile of straw into gold for you?" he asks. "My ring," says the daughter.

In the morning the King comes in.

The little man has spun all the straw into gold. The King
is very pleased. But he's greedy and wants more gold.

He takes the daughter to a bigger room.

There's a bigger pile of straw. "Spin it all by morning,
or you'll die," he says. Soon the little man comes in.

"What will you give me now?" he asks.

"I've nothing left," says the daughter. "Promise to give me your first baby when you're Queen," says the little man.

In the morning, the King is delighted.

"Marry me, and we'll always be rich," he says. Soon
there's a royal wedding and the daughter is the Queen.

The Queen is very happy when her first baby is born.

Then the little man comes. "If you can't guess my name
in three days, I'll take your baby away," he says.

The Queen thinks of names all day and all night.

When the little man comes the next day, she says, "Is it Tom, John or Henry?" The little man says, "No, you're wrong."

The little man comes again the next day.

"Is it Bandylegs, Crooksy or Boggles?" asks the Queen. "No.
One more try and I'll take the baby," says the little man.

The next day, a messenger comes to the Queen.

"I saw a little man in the woods. He was singing, 'My name is Rumpelstiltskin'," he says. "Thank you," says the Queen.

"Your name is Rumpelstiltskin," says the Queen.

The little man is very angry. He stamps the floor so hard, his foot goes through the floor. Then he disappears forever.

This edition first published in 2003 by Usborne Publishing Ltd, 83-85 Saffron Hill, London EC1N 8RT, England. www.usborne.com
Copyright © 2003, 1996 Usborne Publishing Ltd.
The name Usborne and the devices ♀ ⊕ are Trade Marks of Usborne Publishing Ltd. All rights reserved. No part of this publication may be reproduced, stored in a retrieval system, or transmitted in any form or by any means, electronic, mechanical, photocopying, recording or otherwise, without prior permission of the publisher. UE. This edition first published in America in 2004. Printed in Belgium.